Old Harry Rock
and
Tales of the Jurassic Coast

Written by

Barbara Townsend

illustrated by Chantal Bourgonje

Old Harry Rock and Tales of the Jurassic Coast ©2015 Barbara Townsend

The right of Barbara Townsend to be identified as the author of this work has been asserted under the Copyright, Design and Patents Act, 1988.

Second edition published by Savernake Press 2017
First edition published by Savernake Press 2015

ISBN: 978-0-9957039-4-0

Savernake Press, Burbage, Wiltshire SN8 3AN

Website:- www.savernakepress.weebly.com

e-mail:- babstownsend@hotmail.com

Illustrated in Wiltshire by Chantal Marie Bourgonje. www.cfordesign.co.uk

Printed locally by Bulpitt Print Ltd on paper, that is fully recyclable, biodegradable and contains fibre from forests meeting the Forest Stewardship Council principles and criteria (FSC).

Ian Weston
Station Manager-Swanage NCI

Old Harry has been part of my life from the time I joined the National Coastwatch Institution's station at Peveril Point, Swanage nine years ago. We use him to help us estimate the range of ships from our lookout and to check the alignment of the bearing device on our powerful binoculars. Old Harry is 2.2 nautical miles from the lookout on a bearing of 022 degrees.

The lookout is always open to visitors, why not pop in and see Old Harry for yourself?

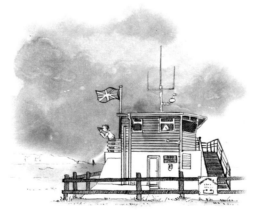

Dinosaurs from the Triassic, Jurassic and Cretaceous periods, from around the world.

triceratops

iguanodon

human

brachiosaurus

tyrannosaurus rex

pteranodon

diplodocus

pliosaur

Acknowledgements

Swanage is an interesting and remarkable place. I have had a great deal of fun researching this book, learnt many new facts and met some wonderful people. This book has been made possible with the help and guidance from the following:-
A massive thank you to -

The National Coastwatch Lookout Station at Peveril Point (for factual content).
The Royal National Lifeboat Institute (RNLI) (for factual content).
The Dorchester Dinosaur Museum (for factual content).
Joy Guy for editing, my grammar is improving!
Chantal Bourgonje, your beautiful illustrations and artwork have brought yet another book to life. We make a great team.
My Granddaughter Issy (age 10) for reading my stories, you are such a great critic and as always I learn something new.
My family, for their continued support and encouragement.
Not forgetting my husband Ian, your belief in me is reassuring. I love you.
Finally to Old Harry, long may you remain standing.

CONTENTS

Old Harry

Old Harry Rock stands sentinel, as though protecting the Jurassic south coast against the onslaught of the sea.

Thousands of years ago, his steep chalk face connected to a land mass joining the Isle of Wight. Previous chalk stacks have succumbed to the sea, their soft chalk walls eventually surrendering to the persistent waves. The remains of Old Harry's wife stand close by, a mere crumbling stump, she collapsed into the sea in 1896, giving in to the sea's relentless attack. Now alone, Old Harry remains strong and bravely fends off the sea's attempts to claim him.

The surrounding chalk, like a sponge, soaks up visions, myths, legends and stories, storing them as memories in the cliffs and deep within the sea bed, like long lost fossils waiting to be dug up and discovered. Struggling to retain the immense force created by the stored energy, Ballard Down bulges. As the years have rolled by, Old Harry has

absorbed the scenes. He has watched as massed galleons and pirate ships sailed across the sea with billowing sails. He stayed silent as smugglers and pirates came to shore, hauling their stolen goods up the cliff face, hiding their loot and themselves from Customs men, who were keen to catch them. He has listened to the whoosh, whoosh sound created by giant turning paddles, propelling steamers with tall colourful chimneys and puffing clouds of steam as they cruised by.

He committed to memory the scenes of horses, pulling stone laden carts into the sea. Men would transfer the large stones onto tiny boats, some far too heavy and awkward for them to lift, ultimately many disappearing into the sea. The stones were cut locally from quarries named Tilly Whim, Winspit and Dancing Ledge. The tiny boats would be rowed precariously out to sea to the waiting ketches anchored offshore, many bound for London.

These precious sought-after stones were used in the building of many prestigious buildings in London and numerous British cathedrals. He has watched as elegant yachts sped silently over the sea, the wind caught in their gigantic sails. He has soaked up the sounds of aircraft noisily chasing the clouds and modern jets streaking high across the blue sky. He can recall the chatter of people's voices, their laughter and their tears.

Immeasurable amounts of images and sounds create an energy force waiting to be released. Old Harry has powers and is capable of tapping into this vast energy resource.

The Lost Seal Pup

A storm had raged through the night. Howling winds brought torrential rain that lashed the coastline violently; lightning flashed across the sky like tongues of flame reaching out to the storm's menacing clouds. No one dared to venture outside; animals sought shelter from the deluge of rain. As the dawn crept slowly across the sky, the storm subsided.

The sea's immense waves were reduced to a rolling swell, bringing to shore a blanket of seaweed that had been torn from its seabed. In the dim morning light and as the dark green carpet crept closer and closer to Old Harry, he heard a cry.

He quickly scanned the floating mass and spotted a creature, clinging to a clump of weed and crying pitifully – a lone seal pup. The youngster had been separated from his mother during the storm. Now exhausted, lost and hungry he struggled to hold on.

Although a good sized pup, he still needed his mother's security and reassurance. She would still be feeding him, even at this age.

"Hang on," Old Harry called out to the pup, "you will be safe soon." Old Harry tapped into his energy and sent out a lasso force around the pup. The pup slowly drifted to shore and hauled his tired, drenched body out of the water. "I can't find my mother," he wailed. "I couldn't keep up with her and the waves were so huge, I couldn't see her." Although distressed and scared, he tried to be brave.

"Don't worry; come and rest and shelter between the rocks and I will attempt to find your mother," Old Harry reassured him. The exhausted pup pulled himself towards the rocks and found a small sandy cave, curled up and fell asleep.

"I must find his mother," Old Harry said quietly, looking at the sleeping pup.

He knew that the mother seal would be looking for the youngster. Crucially, he needed to get a message out into the vast expanse of sea. Old Harry tapped into the energy deep within his cliff face, a power so strong it trembled as it merged with his thoughts.

As the rising power surged, Old Harry focused. He released the energy and the silent message carried deep into the seabed. It raced like electricity along the shore line and would be felt on each ripple and wave and sea creatures would be aware of its pulse and sense its urgency.

The pup slept fitfully, jumping and twitching as though dreaming of his ordeal. He eventually awoke with a jolt. With the sudden realisation of his predicament, alone and extremely hungry, he began to cry and call for his mother.

Old Harry was hopeful that the mother would soon locate the energy source radiating deep within and then follow its path to where the pup now lay. If, however, the mother seal had perished during the night, what would happen to the youngster? How long could he survive without her? Those thoughts he would keep from the pup.

Old Harry needed to distract the pup. "Perhaps a story would help," he thought. He brimmed with knowledge and memories, tales lay deep within his walls and surrounding cliffs, waiting to burst out and be released. Always eager to free some of this power, Old Harry shook with anticipation.

He spoke calmly to the pup trying to keep him distracted. "Would you like a story?" The pup stopped wailing. "Yes please," he said with a sniff. Whilst keeping the silent message steady, Old Harry began.

Long ago there lived a pirate called Harry Paye. He came from Poole. Pirates were plentiful in those days but Harry Paye became one of the most famous. Some believed him to be a greedy pirate and no more than a smuggler and rogue. Others believed him to be brave and daring. He had at one time defended the town of Poole and his country with strength and courage.

The King, Henry IV, trusted him and commanded Harry to prevent ships carrying supplies to rebels who threatened the King. The rebels were determined to knock the King from power and take his crown. During his pirating life, Harry attacked many French and Spanish ships stealing their goods and treasure. Both these countries became so outraged with Harry they decided to take their revenge and so raided Poole in the hope of capturing and killing him. However, Harry fled and the French caught his brother instead. He did not survive.

In their frustration, they burnt parts of the town. Harry became extremely unpopular with the Poole people. To make amends and to avenge his brother's death and with only 15 ships at his command, Harry captured 120 French ships laden with wine, oil, salt and iron and brought his spoils back to Poole as gifts for the town's people.

The town forgave Harry and to this day, to celebrate his intriguing life, every year Poole people dress as pirates in honour of this infamous colourful character.

Old Harry looked at the wide-eyed pup.
"It is said that Harry Paye buried stolen treasure around my cliffs and hid here after raids to prevent being captured. That's maybe why I'm called Harry too."

"Did he actually bury treasure here?" asked the eager pup.
"That is a secret that only Harry Paye and I will ever know," Old Harry whispered.

The anxious mother seal had spent the entire night searching relentlessly, but unsuccessfully, to find her pup. Hour upon hour she had searched vast areas of the sea, swimming into Poole Harbour looking out for him in the shallow water, calling and listening in the hope of finding him.

Her calls were drowned by the howling wind and roaring sea. His cries, too, were torn away and lost in the winds. Knowing he needed to feed drove her on; he would not survive long without her. As the dawn approached, she eventually headed for the shore, too exhausted to continue.

The storm had swept her far along the coast to Studland, a four kilometre long curved sweep of beautiful sandy beaches backed by soft dunes and heathland. Normally, early risers would be jogging or strolling along this popular shoreline.

Luckily, that day, the storm had kept them away; she took the opportunity to rest undisturbed before continuing her search. She sheltered amongst the soft dunes and did her best to rest.

The mother seal sensed it – a force unseen, an energy force she didn't recognise but somehow understood at the same time. Urgency now drove her to swim and find her pup. Her tiredness forgotten, she hurtled into the water and headed out to sea, following a trail, although she had no idea where it would lead.

Like a sixth sense, she allowed her body to follow its path. As she swam, her pace quickened, drawn by the unknown source of energy. She leapt out of the water in hope and excitement.
As she leapt she spotted the white cliffs.

Old Harry spotted the leaping mother. "She's on her way," he said cheerfully to the pup.

The pup stared expectantly out to sea frantically searching the horizon for her.

Without hesitation he dived, crashing into the water and swam speedily

out to sea. The delighted seals swam in tight circles, splashing, leaping and barking noisily, happy to be reunited. The mother seal returned to the cliffs, peering at the shoreline and to where Old Harry stood tall, wondering what force had guided and urged her to this spot.

As the pup watched her, he knew he would keep the powers of Old Harry a secret.

The seals took one last look at the white chalk cliffs and were gone.

Jurassic Coast Rescue

Thomas is tall for sixteen. At home in Germany he attends the gym and plays football and loves any outdoor activity. So he enjoys the freedom his trips to Swanage give him.

On one particular trip he decided to explore the area. As an exchange student at a local school, studying English and Geography, the standing chalk rocks across the bay intrigued Thomas and he became determined to get a closer look at the unusual chalk strata.

One bright spring morning he decided to take a kayak out into the bay to reach Old Harry Rocks, but particularly Old Harry himself, standing brilliantly white in the sunshine. Being athletic and a reasonably strong swimmer, he had little fear of the water, so felt prepared for the trip. With a small rucksack loaded with water and snacks and wearing his lifejacket, he set off.

A bright sunny day with a slight breeze blowing offshore; several windsurfers were already chasing the wind and were zipping across the bay. Swimmers, too, were rounding buoys before heading back to the beach. Only visible by their coloured swimming caps, they appeared to be bobbing along like lost beach balls.

Thomas paddled slowly away from the shore and headed for Old Harry. Although not yet visible, Thomas knew he would soon catch a glimpse of the white chalk stacks proudly standing guard. He paddled through the surf close to the cliff face of Ballard Down. As he rounded the headland, the white chalk walls loomed above him and Pinnacle Rock blocked his view of Old Harry.

As he made his way around the pointed stack, the wind unexpectedly caught him off guard, taking his breath away. Thomas could sense the temperature change as the wind swirled around him. He had to paddle furiously to keep himself on course and upright. The now choppy sea splashed over the nose of his kayak sending sea spray into his face.

Determined to reach Old Harry, he forged on now that he had him in his sights.

"I could head for that sandy area between those rocks," he muttered to himself. As Thomas closed in on Old Harry, a gust of wind caught him sideways and slammed the kayak over, throwing Thomas into the cold sea. Thomas's head hit rocks.

Old Harry had watched amused at the effort Thomas made to reach him. Drastically, with the suddenness of the wind catching him off guard, this young man now lay face up, unconscious and bleeding from his head wound, being kept afloat by his lifejacket.

Old Harry focused on Thomas, sending an energy field out to his floating body. It enveloped him and as Old Harry concentrated, Thomas slowly floated to the shoreline. He became wedged between two rocks which prevented him from drifting back into the chilly water. Thomas moaned and opened his eyes; confused, shaken and in pain, he touched his bruised head and felt the blood. "What's happened?" he murmured looking at his blood.

"You fell out of your kayak and hit your head on rocks," Old Harry replied.
"What? Who said that?" Thomas looked around trying to see where the voice came from. His head hurt as he moved it. "Ouch!" he moaned again.
Thomas floated in and out of consciousness and Old Harry knew he needed help and quickly.

It would require most of Old Harry's strength and concentration to get help. He tapped into the energy stored deep within the chalk, the nearby cliffs and the seabed; he focused hard and drew on its power. He felt it rising, like sap racing up the veins of a tall tree, reaching out to its extreme branches. He felt each pulse and as it surged, waiting to be released to nearly bursting point, he homed in on the National Coastwatch Lookout Station at Peveril Point across the bay and unleashed the power. Like a laser, a continuous beam of light flashed across the bay in an instant.

Two men were on duty at the Station. William, who had been volunteering at the Lookout for nearly 10 years, scanned the horizon with his binoculars.

To his right he could see as far as Durlston, a conservation area enjoyed by the public. Positioned above the Jurassic rocks is Durlston Castle, a refurbished Victorian building. Straight ahead of him and visible on clear days, The Isle of Wight. To his left, he had a magnificent view of Old Harry Rocks and beyond.

He also scanned the coastal paths for walkers who could have slipped and fallen. Jack, a new recruit, checked the weather instruments, collecting data for the Met Office. Both volunteers enjoyed being Watch-keepers and were proud of the vital contribution the Station made, working together with the Royal National Lifeboat Institute (RNLI) and the Search and Rescue helicopter. Monitoring radio channels and logging the movement of commercial and leisure vessels kept many volunteers busy throughout the year at Peveril Point.

Hoping they would spot his signal, Old Harry knew the Lookout Station could help and the Watch-keepers would be on duty.

As William scanned the horizon for overturned boats, distress flares, windsurfers and swimmers in trouble, he spotted the beam of light radiating from Old Harry. "Jack, check this out," he said, pointing toward the rocks across the bay. Jack stared at the light. "Is that a torch? It's not a flare. You know, I'm not sure what that is," he said, squinting at the light.

"It's too bright to make out the source; someone is trying to get our attention, that's for sure," William muttered, still peering through his binoculars. With his years of experience, he immediately rang the Coastguard explaining the unusual light emitting from Old Harry Rock. "It's coming from the shoreline at the base of Old Harry," he explained, "it's a continuous beam and incredibly bright. I've not seen anything like this before; but it's pointing directly at the Lookout Station so someone is trying to get our attention. I will let you know if it changes --- Great, thanks, keep us posted --- They're launching the rescue boat," William said, excitedly.

Old Harry had to focus to maintain the light emitting from his core. He also needed to keep Thomas alert. His head injury could be serious. With Thomas floating in and out of consciousness, he needed to keep him wide awake.

"I have it," Old Harry said after giving it some thought.
It would be tricky keeping the laser light strong and Thomas safe.

However, he felt exhilarated. The thought of being able to unleash a great deal of energy and power helped to keep him focused.

Above Thomas, ghostly images appeared, emerging from the white chalk cliff face - roaring and bellowing dinosaurs. The white cliff face acted like a huge cinema screen for Old Harry to bring the images to life. Thomas became transfixed as he saw Triassic, Jurassic and Cretaceous dinosaurs, in massive herds. From different eras and from around the world they now roamed together. Thomas stared as he saw sauropods; he recognised a Brachiosaurus and a Diplodocus, with their pillar-like legs and their extraordinarily long necks.

Fierce theropods ran together. Many were tiny and ran around like chickens. "A Megalosaurus," muttered Thomas, as one roamed by. However, the most awesome of all theropods, the Tyrannosaurus rex, standing on its powerful hind legs must have been 5 metres tall and over 12 metres long. It had tiny front limbs and claws, however, its huge jaw, full of long serrated teeth, created a powerful weapon, capable of

trapping and killing its prey.

A huge Triceratops lumbered by. This three-horned, plant-eating beast must weigh at least 10 tons, its head alone measuring over 2 metres in length. "Iguana Tooth" Thomas said aloud, as he remembered the meaning of the name Iguanodon, one ran surprisingly fast for its size. This plant-eater weighing over 3.5 tons and 10 meters long had strange conical sharp spikes for thumbs, perhaps to defend itself with.

A Pteranodon swooped from the sky, like a winged lizard with a gigantic wing span of 9 metres. Other tiny pterosaurs flew in flocks. Amazing dinosaurs were everywhere; these creatures he had only read about. So stunned, he could not tear his eyes away.
A huge male Brachiosaurus appeared. It measured practically 30 metres long. This creature that lived around 150 million years ago, towered above Thomas.

As the sauropod bent its immense neck to drink fresh water flowing into the sea, a Pliosaur rocketed out of the sea and sank its huge razor sharp teeth into the sauropod's neck. This massive sea creature lived around 155 million years ago, measuring roughly 18 metres in length, its head, over 2 metres long. The Brachiosaurus screamed in pain. As Thomas watched, these two incredible different creatures were now in a life or death struggle.

Thomas painfully shook his head, convinced he must be dreaming. He could not take his eyes from the battling dinosaurs.

The Coastguard immediately contacted the RNLI in Swanage and sent out a pager alert. Responding, the crew headed for the lifeboat. One volunteer crew member ran along the rocky pathway below the Downs at Peveril Point. Another arrived in her car.

The crew members kitted up and on board the inflatable lifeboat, headed out to Old Harry. They, too, could see the light radiating from the base of his stack. The lifeboat sped across the bay bouncing over the waves. The inflatable is highly manoeuvrable, perfect for operating close to cliffs and well suited to surf and shallow water around the chalk stacks.

As the boat neared Old Harry and the crew spotted Thomas, the beam of light immediately disappeared.

"What was that?" Issy said, as she jumped ashore to reach Thomas. She could see that although conscious, he looked stunned and she noticed the bleeding from his head wound. With her high standard of first aid training, Issy could quickly assess Thomas's needs.

"Hi I'm Issy, what's your name?" she said reassuringly as she reached him. Thomas, although aware of voices, remained transfixed by the battling dinosaurs, not happy at being thrashed around, the pliosaur reluctantly released its grip from around the sauropod's neck, crashed back into the sea and disappeared.

The dinosaur images began to fade as Old Harry regained control of the surging energy, capping it once again. "You'll be fine now," Old Harry whispered softly to Thomas.

"I will be fine now," said Thomas aloud.
"You will," said Issy, tending to his head wound. Her crew mate had radioed for an ambulance to meet them close to the beach. Although Issy had assessed that Thomas had no broken bones, he shivered from

the cold and the shock of his ordeal. He also needed stitches for his head wound. They gently put Thomas into the lifeboat, wrapped in a space blanket keeping him warm.

"Did you lose your safety helmet?" Issy asked, looking around for it.
"I didn't have one," replied Thomas, sheepishly.

As the small inflatable sped over the water heading for the beach and the waiting ambulance, Thomas turned to look at Old Harry Rock, "There were dinosaurs, huge fighting dinosaurs," he said, staring at the white cliffs.

"That will be the bang on the head," Issy replied, smiling at Thomas.

Also available:-

Written by Barbara Townsend
Illustrated by Chantal Bourgonje

'The Savernake Big Belly Oak'

As frightened creatures escape into the safety of Tree's enormous big belly, he comforts them with tales of the forest.
For children 4 to 11 years.

'The Oaks of Savernake and the Legendary Ghosts'

Venerable veteran oak trees stand in the ancient forest of Savernake. Over 1000 years old, many have shrunk under their own great weight and have become wide and gnarly, their immense size bending and twisting them out of shape giving them the appearance of demons and monsters.

They are, however, gentle giants with powers far beyond our understanding.

For children 7 to 11 years.

'Stonehenge – Luke and the Bluestone'

Luke, the main character, is a 15 year old school boy, is not keen on the idea of a school trip to 'some old stones'!! With a twist of past and present Luke, is unwittingly placed amongst the very people transporting one of the mighty Bluestones from West Wales to Wiltshire. Travelling with them, they experience some of the emotions and extremes of human effort that must have gone into building one of mankind's singular and most remarkable achievements.

For children 8 to 12 years.

'Harriet'

Harriet dares to be different. The unseen force that drives her and the colony disappears, leaving the bees confused and vulnerable. Their lives devastated by a deadly attack, this brave honey bee leads a group to safety and journeys to find a new home and her destiny.

For children 7 to 11 years

www.savernakepress.weebly.com

babstownsend@hotmail.com